The Revolt

A Revolt in Yemen

The Revolt

A Revolt In Islamabad

Stephen J Rand

The Revolt

Of the Dharma Chakras

A Murder in the Amazons

The Tempest in Tibet

A Novel

THE

REDEMPTION

YEMEN

Beki Jr - The Ruler of Africa

Introduction

On the 26th of March 2015, Saudi Arabia and a coalition of Arab states began 'Operation Decisive Storm,' launching their first airstrike against the Houthi in Yemen This marked the most recent stage in the transformation of Yemen's ongoing internal struggles with Houthi uprisings, into a war involving military actors from outside of its territory. Following the Houthi takeover of the capital Sana'a in September 2014, the already fragile and instable state collapsed into a civil war (BBC 2015). As the Houthi continued to gain greater territory and control President Hadi was forced to flee, first to Aden in the south and eventually to Saudi Arabia, at which time he personally requested an intervention to halt the Houthi advance. By responding to his call, Saudi Arabia brought itself deeper into the discourse surrounding the conflict, and in doing so emphasized what it saw as the disruptive role played another regional power; Iran. As such, the conflict in Yemen has been viewed as a new front in the struggle between Saudi Arabia and Iran

Republic of Yemen was formed in 1990, and has an estimated population of 26 million people, 99,1 % of which are Muslim. A 65% majority of these are Sunni, the remaining 35% are Shia (CIA 2016). The current conflict has exasperated the country's economic difficulties and a staggering 82%

of the population is thought to require humanitarian assistance (CIA 2016). It is the poorest country in the Arab region UNOCHA 2016), with more than half of the population living below the poverty line (CIA 2016).

Prologue

Beki checked his Rolex watch; it was evening 5 pm, so they have to try to get in by 2 am .That was the time when the President retires for rest and would not be disturbed till early morning. They knew the President resided in the north eastern part of the building, ground stairs. His House is heavily guarded from all sides with tall electrocuted walls. Inside were the elite forces and ferocious dogs with surveillance cameras everywhere. So practically it was impossible to take him on. Kabila and Langa had now left the city's main line of the sewerage tank and made their way into sewerage line the President's House. Their hard work made it easier for us to follow.

There were two lines one for water and one for human excreta. The line carrying out the human excreta was broad enough for one man to move. After hours of hard digging, they finally reached the area just below the wash room they thought was the President's suit. They opened the fittings with their multipurpose knife slowly moved up into the floor. It was 3 am. They looked at the compass and knew they were spot on. Through the see through night Vision goggles they saw the President was sleeping, alone. His family was already in Paris sensing trouble. They slowly opened the door connecting the President's room and slid in. A dose of strong chloroform did enough for the President to pass away. Their back journey was very tedious carrying thebigman. It took them seven hours to reach the point, where they could come out. In the meanwhile, the elite guards, when they opened the doors to the President's House, could not fathom what could have happened. Had the President fled the country in secrecy? His close associates were all confused and doubted the other group to have assisted the President to escape.

They were perplexed at the turn of events. They called a meeting of all the top officials that supported the President's government, the ministers, chief of the army, and other important officials, to take decisions on the future of their government. They were having their meeting in the Presidential suite when a thundering explosion brought the building down along with all the occupants. The explosion was loud enough to be heard by Beki

Soon enough the deposed President - came on the National Television and announced he had fled to France and asked members to surrender! That was enough- over night he became a traitor – which he was! Suddenly the war stopped! Many lives were saved.

Chapter

Sanna - On the fateful day the President was invited to lunch at the house of his vice-president Al-Ghashmi. The invitation was made to look like a last-minute casual invitation and most of the invited guests were either ministers or close friends of Al-Ghashmi. Upon his arrival, Al-Hamdi was taken into a room where he found his General Beki - Dead. Some have suggested that President Al-Hamdi may have tried to dissuade his would-be assassins from their plan by proposing to resign. However, the conspirators were likely frightened of Al-Hamdi's unshakable popularity among Yemenis who would have taken to the streets had Al-Hamdi resigned. Both Al-Hamdi and his supporters were killed in cold blood. Bottom of Form

Al-Ghashmi, Al-Hamdi's vice president, was obviously a key suspect in the deaths. Because the killing took place at his home at his personal invitation to Al-Hamdi and his rapid assumption of power left little doubt of his evil role in the assassination plot. Also a rival group of army officers had convinced the Saudis that Al-Hamdi's approach toward South Yemen was dangerous to their mutual interests and sought the Saudi's consent, if not their support. Incongruously, Mr. Ransom discredited the idea that the Saudis were directly involved in the assassination plot although he may have simply meant they did not actually fire the weapons.

Can the General's Son Beki Jr Avenge his father's death as well as restore, peace and stability among the warring African Nations!

Chapter

The highlands of Taiz were Beki's homeland. And therefore he has chosen it as the base for their revolt against the evil – de facto Ruler! Zed and Prince had joined him. The historic Cairo Castle Taiz for the last six months has been used as a barracks, to train local volunteers. Beki was joined by his brothers in arms – MO Hawk , Adwait and Prince.

Taiz is the capital and Beki's Village was under that governorate. Taiz   is a city in southwestern Yemen .

 It is located in the Yemeni Highlands, near the port city ofMocha on theRed Sea , lying at an elevation of about 1,400 metres (4,600 ft) above sea level. It is the capital of Taiz . Taiz is considered to be the cultural capital of Yemen n 130 CE the Jewish quarters was established in the city. One of the famous and most accepted traveler in Taiz was Ibn Battuta. In his travels he describes this city as "one of the most beautiful and extensive cities of Yemen." Ibn was invited to a banquet with the king and received a warm and inviting welcome.

The city has many old and beautiful quarters, with houses that are typically built with brown bricks, and mosques are usually white. Most famous among the mosques are the Ashrafiya , theMuctabiya and theMudhafir. Also memorable are the old citadel and the governor's palace that rests on top of a mountain spur 450 metres above the city centre.

It also has one of the most famous mountains in Yemen, the Saber mountain (almost 3000 meters above sea level), which affords panoramic views over the city. The city has a Muslim madrasa that has university status. Historically, the mountainous city of Taiz was known for coffee and cheese production The coffee produced in Taiz was considered some of the finest in the region in the early 20th century.

Beki and Sanaa our country's Capital is one of the oldest continuously inhabited cities in the world, although an exact date for its establishment is unknown. According to Yemeni legend, **i**t was founded by Shem, one of the three sons of Noah . It occupies the site of the ancient pre-Islamic stronghold of Ghumdān, which may date to the 1st and 2nd century BCE. Sanaa was an Arabian centre for Christians and Jews before it was converted to Islam by Ali , fourth caliph and son-in-law of the Prophet Muhhamad, in 632 CE.

Prince – Very impressive history . And what a sorry state of affairs , Yemen is the most dangerous place in the world for travelers

Beki – Unfortunately ! But Yemen under President Ibrahim Muhammad Al-Hamdi was a highly progressive state - after his murder – Yemen is not the same again.

Beki – My father along with former President were murdered in cold blood. North Yemen's charismatic President Ibrahim Muhammad Al-Hamdi was mysteriously murdered in Sana'a . President Ibrahim Al-Hamdi', trusted associate BEKI , my father who also served as a top military general in Yemen, was also killed together with him.   Al-Hamdi's government embarked on ambitious economic development plans to help bring North Yemen closer to 20th century modernity. Al-Hamdi worked vigorously to establish the rule of law in a country torn by a decade of civil war. Within a very short period of time, Al-Hamdi gained the political trust of an overwhelming majority of Yemeni citizens at home and abroad.

However, there was a small group of tribal leaders and military officers who felt threatened by Al-Hamdi's policies and increasing popularity. They saw the building of modern state institutions and the application of the rule of law as a danger to the existing structure of political power. Shaikh Abd Allah Hussein Al-Ahmar opposed Al-Hamdi from his stronghold tribal center in Khamir. Moreover, Al-Hamdi's personal appeal to the leaders of South Yemen greatly concerned the Saudis, who viewed the socialist regime in the south as an existentialist threat. It thus came as no surprise that Al-Hamdi was killed on the eve of his visit to President Salim Rubai Ali in Aden.

On the fateful day the President was invited to lunch at the house of his vice-president Al-Ghashmi. The invitation was made to look like a last-minute casual invitation and most of the invited guests were either ministers or close friends of Al-Ghashmi. Upon his arrival, Al-Hamdi was taken into a room where he found his General Beki - Dead . Some have suggested that President Al-Hamdi may have tried to dissuade his would-be assassins from their plan by proposing to resign. However, the conspirators were likely frightened of Al-Hamdi's unshakable popularity among Yemenis who would have taken to the streets had Al-Hamdi resigned. Both Al-Hamdi and his supporters were killed in cold blood. MO Hawk so it was a pre-planned attempt by the Vice President and of course others who were fearful for his popularity. Beki Al-Ghashmi, Al-Hamdi's vice president, was obviously a key suspect in the deaths. Because the killing took place at his home at his personal invitation to Al-Hamdi and his rapid assumption of power left little doubt of his evil role in the assassination plot. Also a rival group of army officers had convinced the Saudis that

Al-Hamdi's approach toward South Yemen was dangerous to their mutual interests and sought the Saudi's consent, if not their support. Incongruously, Mr. Ransom discredited the idea that the Saudis were directly involved in the assassination plot although he may have simply meant they did not actually fire the weapons.

Abd Al-Baree Itwan, a London-based Palestinian journalist, admitted in a rare TV interview following the Yemeni uprisings that President Saleh once confessed to him in Sana'a that he took power in Yemen through the use of force while removing his personal curved blade dagger (Janbiya) from its sheath. Many Yemenis took this statement as an indication of Saleh's role in the assassination of Al-Hamdi. For many Yemenis, Saleh's vehement efforts to eliminate all references to Al-Hamdi from Yemen's public life and refusal to allow any official investigation of his assassination speaks volumes about Saleh's probable involvement. Sa*ana* the capital city of Yemen.

Chapter

As they reached the outskirts of the city they found it was heavily barricaded. Mo Hawk understood that their only way to win the war was to engage them in hand to hand combat so he decided they had to move fast. The city had two main entrances, one from the north and the other from the west. There was also a narrow bridge over the canal that connected the Southern part of the city. As there was no surprise element in the fighting the rebels had to fight from brick by brick. By evening the first attack was on. A missile came straight in and exploded in the rebel's camp with a deafening sound, instantly killing a dozen of their men. It followed by several others.

The rebels led by Beki and MO Hawk had gathered in the outskirts ! They had decided on an alternative plan. They already engaged the army in the northern side and making their way into the city. Fierce one to one fighting ensued.

In the western side Prince and Adwait were pressing forward with their group. The peasant's forces were behind them to back up. The fighting waged on for a month and there was no sign of the regime falling.

 But the good news was the people of the city were supporting the rebels and thousands of peasants were moving from the surrounding villages towards the city.

Mo Hawk and Beki understood that something had to done fast or else if the struggle continued for long it will be disadvantageous for them. So they planned to attack the Presidential house. There were two local guerrillas Kabila and Langa who were aware of the city planning as they were the elite guards of the late President, and knew the details of the Presidential House like the back of their hand.

Beki thought they were lucky to have them in their ranks.

While fighting raged on between the rebels and the President's forces on the streets of the city, Beki , Mo Hawk along with Kabila and Langa were making their way through the underground sewerage system. Their progress was slow but steady and as they had no communication system to contact for guidance they were on their own; however the compass was good enough to lead them in the right direction It took them seven hours to reach a place underneath the President's house. They checked their oxygen masks it would not last for long. They had to make their entry as quickly as possible.

Beki checked his Rolex watch; it was evening 5 pm, so they have to try to get in by 2 am .That was the time when the President retires for rest and would not be disturbed till early morning. They knew the President resided in the north eastern part of the building, ground stairs. His House is heavily guarded from all sides with tall electrocuted walls. Inside were the elite forces and ferocious dogs with surveillance cameras everywhere. So practically it was impossible to take him on. Kabila and Langa had now left the city's main line of the sewerage tank and made their way into sewerage line the President's House. Their hard work made it easier for us to follow.

There were two lines one for water and one for human excreta. The line carrying out the human excreta was broad enough for one man to move. After hours of hard digging, they finally reached the area just below the wash room they thought was the President 's suit . They opened the fittings with their multipurpose knife slowly moved up into the floor. It was 3 am. They looked at the compass and knew they were spot on. Through the see through night Vision goggles they saw the President was sleeping, alone. His family was already in Paris sensing trouble. They slowly opened the door connecting the President's room and slid in. A dose of strong chloroform did enough for the President to pass away. Their back journey was very tedious carrying thebigman. It took them seven hours to reach the point, where they could come out. In the meanwhile, the elite guards, when they opened the doors to the President's House, could not fathom what could have happened.

Had the President fled the country in secrecy? His close associates were all confused and doubted the other group to have assisted the President to escape.

They were perplexed at the turn of events. They called a meeting of all the top officials that supported the President's government, the ministers, chief of the army, and other important officials, to take decisions on the future of their government. They were having their meeting in the Presidential suite when a thundering explosion brought the building down along with all the occupants. The explosion was loud enough to be heard by Beki

Soon enough the deposed President - came on the National Television and announced he had fled to France and asked members to surrender! That was enough- over night he became a traitor – which he was! Suddenly the war stopped! Many lives were saved.

It was a matter of time, for the rebels to take over the main city. The rebels, peasants, city dwellers all rejoiced throughout the night. At last evil had fallen. In the morn many important decisions were taken. There was a paradigm shift in the rebels thought process, instead of hanging the deposed President, as was the custom, they sent him to a prison in a friendly country, where he shall be tried in the fairest way. The Rebels and the peasants voted Beki to take over the governance of the nation. Though he was reluctant, on The elders of the various tribes , who had lent him support , to fight the evil , unanimously persuaded him to take

over the reins of the Country !
Kabila and Langa became his trusted
lieutenants in ruling the nation.
There was a coronation ceremony,
where all the Chiefs of Africa
attended to support him. And it was a
happy reunion for Beki and his
family, his three mothers and his
sisters! Beki made his Capital City -
Taiz , his home state and he ruled
from the Governor's Palace.

They missed their proud father. He
was now the official head of his family
and the owner of his father's
legendary Gun and the Sword! And
he knew now it was his turn to tell his
father's tales – both real and unreal!

Chapter

Today would be an extra-ordinary day for the young Beki, as his life would change forever. When the young Beki, got up   from bed, he found his three mothers and their father outside, standing by the front gate. When he strolled up to their side, his two elder sisters were already there. So were the neighbors, all at their gates.AS he looked on he saw a strange sight, people atop open vans with big guns, were passing by and the vans were never ending! And he had not seen so many white men at one time. His father informed them that they were the foreign mercenaries fighting for the New President Obumba's regime. The new regime had come to power after assassinating the popular regime that had come to power after overthrowing the foreign rule. The President Sholke- Al-Hamdi's was the first President after their independence. And Beki's father had been one of the revolutionaries who had fought for his country's freedom. And now everything has gone in vain. The supporters of

Sholke Al-Hamdi's had started a counter revolution to take revenge. The whole of Africa was in chaos, it was obvious that the imperial powers along with their local partners were after Ivory, gold, oil and now diamonds. Tribal cleansing betweentwo groups has resulted in millions of deaths and millions of children rendered homeless. There are more than 2, 00,000 child soldiers in Africa right now. One can understand the white's exploiting the

Africans, but you can't understand what their own people are doing to them. One can say God has left Africa long ago. The story of Africa has been a story of exploitation first the slave traders , then the colonists and the imperialists the Dutch, Belgians, French, Italians, the English had a free for all of Africa's resources. After the revolutions we a saw a spurt of Independent democratic Nations , but due to their inexperience and corruption the democratic set ups failed giving way to military rule and dictatorships and followed by assassinations and leaders leaving their countries to take up asylum in foreign nations, France has been a favorite hideout. Well the new regime was being supported by one of the super powers and the previous imperial nation that had occupied their nation. So to counter them the supporters of late President Sholke, had requested the support of the peasant masses that had fought for him to overthrow the foreign rule as well as they had called the World Guerrilla Association , headed by Fuser who was an Argentinean, but fought with the Cubans Guerrillas successfully. After Cuba's freedom He had set up a world body of Guerrillas to counter and oppose imperial and oppressive rule in Latin

America, Africa, Europe and Asia. All had been quite for quite some while. After fighting the war to free their country Beki's father was a hero, in their village. His father was a great swords man and gunman. Unlike other Africans he had adjusted to the new Maxim guns and was devastating on the enemy ranks. How many heads he had rolled he had lost count. In a bitterly fought war they had won.

The famous Gun hung proudly hung in the wall of his father's room. Villagers would often come around in the evening and share goshup – the village wine from the Palm trees and they would be treated to yams and sometimes meat along with the wine as his father would revel them with his heroics in the war. And the partying continued to the wee hours of morning. The drunk neighbors would return back to warm their waiting wives, and also tell them the stories of his father's exploits. It was a privilege for the village folks to spend time with his father.Of course his father was almost a living legend. Though he had been offered a decent job by the government, he had declined and returned back to his village to lead a peaceful life. And peaceful it was. After coming back rich he could afford two more marriages. So he had three wives and three children by them. Two girls and one son Beki.

He had ten big fields where he cultivated Yam. He had Oxen and cattle, goats and poultry which gave eggs. And eggs were a rarity in their village. His house was at the front. At the backside were three big huts each belonging to his three wives? And at their back were the Yam fields, the sheds for cattle, goats and the oxen. The poultry sheds were built adjoining his wives huts. Each of the wives cooked their own food separately and provided for food to their father during breakfast, lunch and dinner and could only eat after his father had eaten. While his father ate he would tell them war stories, some real and some unreal. His mother's liked each other and spent time gossiping and tending to each other. They were very hard working both in the house as well as in the fields. When there were wrestling matches or sword fighting in the ILO or the village play grounds , his father would take all of them to watch the action. And young Beki being the boy of the house would beallowed to take his father's stool, on which his father would sit and watch. His father was a proud man and was much respected in his village and the adjoining villages not only for his valor in the war but also for taking up three wives, signifying that he was a wealthy man. In important events his father was always the guest of honor. And in village conflicts he was the unofficial judge. All was well till this fateful day!

At night fall three African's along with a white man slipped into his father's room. He was surprised as never had a white man walked into their house. They had a long conversation and there no wine or party but they were doing some serious discussions. Now there were around three hours to dawn and his father summoned his wives and the young Beki to his room. He informed them that war had once again resumed and he had to leave immediately to join the rebels and he would be the head of the zone under which their own village would fall. So he told them he will try to be in touch with them whenever possible. He addressed young Beki as the head of the household and asked him to take care of his house in his absence. The thought of war made his thighs to tremble and his body rushed up with fire and he trembled with desire to conquer and overpower. It was like the desire for woman. Kissing his family good bye he left with the men waiting for him outside. As they bid him from the gates slowly his father and his companions turned away from them and faded into the darkness.

Chapter

 Soon enough battles ensued among the forces of slain President Sholke and the De facto, President Odumbe. The whole nation was in fire. The rebels had captured the northern hills and were staging their guerrilla movement from the mountains. Young Africans were being recruited and trained under the Argentina Guerrilla leader Fuser and his companions from Latin America. The Guerrillas mingled with the local populace and started the process of orientation, educating them about the de facto misrule that was selling out resources to the foreign powers. The Guerrillas met the people working in the mines, and apprised them of the loss of national resources, which belonged to them but is being dished to the neo- imperial masters. It was necessary to educate them and get their support because without the support of the local people Guerrilla warfare will fail as it did in Bolivia. After training the young Guerrillas and getting the support of the local people the rebels moved to the next stage. They sent small groups to various parts of the country and controlled small pickets, slowly surrounding the defacto regime from all sides. The small groups of Guerrillas started attacking government installations. Mines and Oil depots were attacked; transport lines were cut off from the capital. Export activities came to a standstill. Business establishments also suffered from the constant fighting between the rebels and the de facto government. The de facto Presidents armed forces retaliated by rampaging village after village, burning the houses, raping the women, lining up the young men and shooting them point blank and they took away the children with them to use them as human shields against the rebels. We have seen Guerrillas carrying out such activities, but the government forces carrying out such genocide against their own   people were hard to believe. Really as someone said, "God had left Africa long back". By these acts they were distancing themselves from their own people. In one such raid, the government forces attacked Beki's village. It was afternoon when the drum beaters sounded the alarming sounds and the villagers gathered at the ILO the village playground. The village elders were informed the marauding troops were only five villages away and drum beaters had informed them that they had raged whole villages and had murdered whole populations, raping women and maiming children. They knew that they did not have the power to fight the armed forces, especially with their spears and swords against Maxim Guns. In traditional warfare they were heroes but in front of the guns they would face slaughter. So they decided that they must retreat to the nearby hills, as that was their last resort, and they knew the armed forces will not be able follow them there. So the villagers made fast to the hills with whatever they could carry with themselves. For they knew if they saved their lives today they would live to take revenge another day.

No sooner had the villagers had fled to the hills the marauders reached the village and started incessant shooting with their machine guns. They raged the whole village as the villagers watched in dismay, their ancestral houses being destroyed. All their traditional houses and houses of gods were raged to the ground. These rascals will definitely one day pay for all this. Though they were feeling sorrowful at their great loss, yet in a way they were happy that their lives and their children's lives had been saved. When Beki reached his village a week after, the villagers was still in the hills too terrified to come down to the village. He was delighted to find his family alive as he had feared for the worst. He knew the elders had taken the right decision, in fleeing to the hills. The elders were against settling in the village as they knew a fresh attack was not far away. And in a way they had adjusted to the hills, they were of the view that only after the civil war it will be safe for them to return back to their village and build their homes again

Chapter

However, Beki had already taken the decision to take his family away from this civil war to safety. That evening he left with his family, his three wives, and two daughters and the Young Beki. He had two companions with him who strongly built and were his body guards. As they started on their journey they knew it would be a long journey, through hard terrain, forests and high hills. They had to take a detour avoiding the roads which were manned by the government troops. They camped in the day and travelled in the darkness of night so that their movement would not be found out. The hard walking made them weary and tired and they would doze off in the safety of natural caves in the day time. They were living on the Yam they had carried with them, they did not hunt as they could not start a fire. Beki carried a compass with him which he used from time to time to be sure of the direction I which they were going .He taught the young Beki to use it , and he was very fascinated by it. As they were moving only by night, their movement was rather slow. For Young Beki and his sisters it was an awakening ,till just a few days back their whole world was restricted to their village and a couple of other villages , and the hills but now they were amazed as well as shocked to find out that the world did not end there.

But there was a beautiful world outside. No wonder their life was on the verge of a radical change. It took them seven days and nights to reach a place that was some kind of a border, manned by troops. As they neared the gates, a tall man in army fatigue came forward to embrace his father and welcomed him in the African language.

He was Emilio, Fuser's second in command. Now they were in a friendly country and they had crossed the borders safely. Beki's family was taken to a safe house where they are to stay. Beki's sisters were admitted to the St Mary's Christian School. And Beki decided to send the young Beki, on Fuser's advice to the City of Buenos Aires for further studies.

The rebel s struggle carried on for several years! They had reached a critical stage . They were having a core meeting in a remote village- as the usually did –but today was different – unknown to them – the Presidents Elite Force had already, surrounded the Village! Some insider's job. Sr Beki and his core members realizing there was no escape , put sword to themselves and died .

Chapter

They followed a loose Aristocratic system; where the 12 Chieftains of the 12 provinces were part of his Cabinet to aid and advise him in ruling the nation. Besides, for the time the chieftainship was hereditary but eventually they would be elected. Through popular ballot. Democracy had failed to take roots in Africa and the Latin America, because for thousands of years they have been ruled by small kings or chieftains, successfully, so when we thrust democracy on them it eventually does not work, as they are not a matured society like the Britain, where we know that democracy took roots gradually through hundreds of years, USA declared itself a democratic state because they carried the experience of England and France with them. India also had a tradition of Kingship Rule

Coming back to Africa Beki decided to run the government in the traditional way that they have been successfully doing since thousands of years. They were against importing western systems.

So Beki along with his 12 senior advisors were the legislature. The legislators could also be women. They had junior officials who executed their plans and looked after general administration. 12 old men were nominated from the 12 provinces to form the Supreme Court and each province had 12 nominated senior men as judges in the Provincial court. In the village level the village chief, along with three nominated elders acted as judges. One of the members had to be a woman. Under the new government the nation started reconstruction works to restore peace and stability in the country.

And their model was followed by the other African nations. As for his family, his wives and daughters were united with him, and they went on stay in the temporary guest house, put up for them. As for MO Hawk as his work was completed he prepared to leave. His next target was the nations of Latin America. Before leaving he laid down certain rules and regulation for the governance of the Nation. His hand book provided for the structure of the state which shall have seven components. The Ruler, The officials, the armed forces, the people, a rich treasury, economic activity, and allies. He opined that a strong state with a strong President (Ruler) was the first requirement for any state because without a strong King there will be the rule of the jungle. A King who is wise, disciplined, devoted, to a just governing of the subjects and conscious of the welfare of all beings will enjoy the earth unopposed. In their happiness is his happiness; in their welfare is his welfare. Old African saying

- **The   President –** Responsibilities   :   Palana ,Rakshana, Yogashema,
- The President shall be fair to the just and use power to punish the wrongdoer
- President or benevolent King shall not have absolute power but be governed by law and advised by the senior advisors.

The Officials – senior advisors and executives – selected on merit.

The armed forces – strong enough to deter terrorist groups and rebellions.

The people- should get their basic needs fulfilled food, house, health, opportunity to income and education.

A rich treasury – makes a strong King. **Economic activity**, Common currency for Africans and common utilization of markets and commodities- resources.

Allies. Comity of African nations not through meetings but through football matches!

Chapter

It was the Summer of his 24 th year ! He graduated! In a way he was pleased to complete his medical degree in the university of Buenos Aires and was intending to return home and take care of the health situation in Africa It was evening , he had left for his residence.

There was a knock on his door . .But he was surprised when he found a monk standing at his door - along with his fathers friend , he instantly knew something is wrong!

I opened the Door and they came in , and I asked them to sit down . My fathers friend took a packet and opened it - it   was my father's legendary Sword and his Gun. He has asked me to hand it over to you —

and he said you are now the man of the house! I nearly choked with tears and disbelief – how such a legendary warrior could die .And I came to know he was murdered through treachery!

I was felt with remorse and vengeful – he was my strength! I wanted to go back to avenge my father's death. But I knew it was not the right time. But I resolved to myself one day I will go back to avenge my father's death.

They congratulated him on his qualifying as a Doctor, and they said he had to make an important journey before coming home. He was told that he will shortly have visitors who shall escort him on his journey. Soon they left.

Not long after, two monks visited him in his hostel in the wee hours. After seeing them he immediately recognized them, they were the ones who always came in his dream and talked about some secret journey to an unknown kingdom. Without wasting much time they left for the airport - on the onwards journey to the Himalayas!

THE

REDEMPTION

Muzaffarabad

Rumblings In Pakistan

The Facts

May 2007 Bhutto asked for additional assistance from foreign contracting agencies –Blackwater- founded by former navy seal - Erik prince , north Carolina – hired by Cia and Amor – group, London Noel Phillip CEO

Dec 27 2007 Liaquat National Bagh Toyota Land Cruiser. a gun shot hit her neck and another her chest and then detonated the explosives he was wearing. 18.16 pm declared dead at Rawalpindi General Hospital. Mustafa Abu al – Yazidi –claimed responsibility; we terminated the most precious American assets.

Senator latif khosa – reported that she was planning to divulge evidence of fraud in the upcoming elections.

Bhutto's trusted body guard – Shahensha - gunned down in Karachi was also a prime suspect .

Al- Qaeda – Taliban head Baitullah Mehsud .Was killed in a drone attack. Mehsud denied saying tribal people have their own customs . We don't strike women.

After Bhutto s death, supporters wept and broke the hospitals glass doors, threw stones at cars and chanted Dog Musharraf , dog. Demonstrations were wide spread in Pakistan – in Peshawar, Multan, Sindh, Karachi - Bhutto's home city. Musharraf ordered a crackdown on rioters and looters to ensure security. The railways were destroyed . The railways suffered a pkr 12.3 billion. The houses and offices of politicians, local government mayors and administration were the victims of mass reaction

support of rogue intelligence agents –
support of local police – Khurram Shahzad /
Rawalpindi police chief Saud Aziz

Mussaraf - was the man behind the
assassination – and all evil elements
conspired to kill her! The Army had their
agenda, the Al Qeada - , Taliban , the
religious extremists ! She was murdered in
Rawapindi - The HQ of Pakistan Army.

The Redemption

Location , the hills adjoining Muzaffarabad , Azad Kashmir . Time 5 Pm.

Adwait and Prince had been waiting for this opportunity for a long time. They had recruited locals who had sworn to them of secrecy. They knew if the General can be disposed – all the other will fall into line! Already there were fissures in the army! HE had usurped power long back and it was popular belief he put all the nation's money in banks in Shangai.

Adwait - we have heard that he was responsible for your mother' s murder .

Prince : Of Course ! I still remember - how she was on election campaigning and she was bombed and shot.

Prince : My mother was the most Charismatic leader, in Asia, she was an Alumni of Oxford University and under my Grand Father , was groomed to rule our Country. After coming to power with absolute majority she brought order and peace, instead of instability and war. And the General was not amused, there is little doubt of his evil role in the assassination plot.

A rival group of army officers had convinced the Chinese that my mother's approach towards India and was dangerous to their mutual interests and sought the consent, if not their support. Incongruously, A Pakistani, a London-based Journalist, admitted in a rare TV interview following the bloody assassination once confessed to

him in the General role in the assassination
– along with the extremist groups whom he
used to carry out his orders!

.NEWS On Dawn Television

Pakistan's General , who was the de facto
President has been killed by Baloch rebels
near the Hills of Muzaffarabad , the Capital
City of POK , a development expected
to implications for the war in the Arab
world's and Afghanistan .

The death was first announced by the a sr Journalist from GEO TV

His assassination was later confirmed to Al Jazeera . Footage circulating on social media appeared to display a body resembling the General , with one video showing how Baloch Rebels militia members used a blanket to move the corpse into the back of a pick-up truck. Sources said he was killed by the rebels in a rocket-propelled grenade and shooting attack on his car at a checkpoint outside Muzzaffarabad.

In a statement read out on the interior ministry announced the "killing" of "General and his supporters".

"This is after he and his men blockaded the roads and killed civilians in a clear collaboration with the enemy countries of the coalition," the statement said.

The ministry also said rebel **forces had** "taken over all the positions and strongholds of the treacherous militia in the capital, Rawalpindi, and the surrounding areas, as well as other provinces in order to impose security".

Sources close to the General – De Facto President told Al Jazeera that the head of the former president's security detail, Raheel Sharif , was among those killed, but did not provide further details.

Chapter

Elsewhere , It Was late into the night and Prince , along with Adwait had reached a small place called Neel am Valley. Which is in the northern most region and district of Azad Kashmir in Pakistan. Thanks to their local guide Hamza Khalid , a resident of Azad Kashmir. There was a small rivulet which they crossed – and into Indian Territory. They knew they had to take a detour through the mountains ranges and passes to reach Hemis , instead of travelling to Sri Nagar ! They had a spring on their toes –mission accomplished. After a somewhat adventurous trek, having successfully maneuvered many trails and difficulties, they finally reached the 3500 meter high Zoji-la pass on the natural border between the valley of Kashmir and the arid lunar landscape of Ladakh. At the top there was a small water body – the size of a bathtub- .The water was warm though the surrounding climate was extremely hostile. The freezing winds were dashing into their bodies – the presence of warm water was definitely some kind of magic by the grace of the lord and carried on refreshed.

Chapter

He snapped awake from his dream. Sweat-drenched, fever-hot, bone-chilled, springing from his mahogany bed, barefoot on the cold red stone floor. Mousier in hand, never out of reach, a sense of security in his fist. Taut muscles, supple limbs, his super sensitive sense instantly attuned to the slightest hint of threat. He scanned the moonlight expanse of his bed chamber with the sharpness of a panther with the scent of stag in its nostrils. Barely seconds after rising from deep sleep, was he ready to take on a dozen armed men or worse. But the bed chamber was empty. The moon was a crescent tonight and the room was caught in a silvery net, more than sufficient for his trained eyes to scan the royal princely apartment. The far wall, some twenty yards from where he stood, showed him a pale imitation of his own reflection in an oval mirror framed in solid gold. A distinct dynastic resemblance, unmistakably related to one of those towering portraits of "his illustrious ancestors adorning the wall of Sultan's hall. Classically handsome, a fitting heir to the dynasty of the Sultan's'- taken after his mother's side. His piercing brown eyes, as sharp and all seeing as a kite-hawk's thousand-yard gaze, scoured every square inch, as he traversed the apartment with quick military precision, his movement graceful and flowing. Bed chamber clear, Gymnasium clear, bathing chambers clear, lobby clear. No intruder sighted circuit complete. Return to bed chamber. Breathing in show rhythms', he extended a martial asana that was part attack and part mental discipline. A few breathtakingly graceful leaps, took him to the old fashioned British style huge verandah with Roman style pillars built by ZB his Grand Father. No sight of his personal guards. His eyes scoured the lobby below through the stairs and the glass hangings from the dome shaped roof above painted on it was the Last Supper, he could never understand how it came to stay there as they were devout Muslims. One day he shall know. Slowly and stealthily he alighted towards the lobby-the main door was locked from inside. Outside he could see a group discussing pensively. Something had happened to "ABBA". He has to reach the Governors house -Where Abba was campaigning .He took a stroll and within minutes reached the GuV S house , surrounded by his father's supporters.

Life has not been very kind to him in the last 5 years. He hailed from a family which was built   on selfless service and sacrifice. His maternal grandfather the great ZB was the ruler who ushered   in democracy in his country -Which was ravaged by military misrule. Of course he became ruler by default as the army along with the general were badly mutilated after facing a humiliating defeat at the hands of its neighboring nation, which was ruled by a strong woman ruler.

"Prince!" Asif's voice was hoarse but the panic in his tone was unmistakable. Asif sat up in bed, sweat pouring down his face, hands sorting out desperately as if trying to grasp someone out of reach.

Prince, be careful! The assassin'. Zarine, his niece was the first to reach his side, simply because she was closer, Prince had snapped awake the instant Asif uttered the first cry. But he was reclining in the baithak – stance across the room and the comfortable nook had lulled him into a fitful doze. He blinked himself awake as he joined his cousin Zarine beside the ex-pm's bedside.

Prince, Asif's face contorted in a look of utter futility and despair. He clenched his fists tight and slammed them down weakly on his thighs. His body shuddered and he bent over, weeping. Zarine

offered a cloth to catch his tears ,and was shocked to find them searing hot .the EX-PM was still burning with fever .It was just a dream, "She said caressing his shoulder , trying to soothe him ,just a bad dream .'He turned jaundiced eyes on her."A dream?"

'Yes, Abba. Prince sat by Asif's feet massaging them gently. 'Just fever dream?

Asif looked down at himself, then at his surrounding as if becoming aware for the first time of where he was.' A dream,' he repeated dully, then pressed the head of his palms into his eyes –giving out a sigh of despair .He was worried as negative thoughts exploded into his brain , stirring it. He cried out in pain. He was worried that his thoughts might become a prophesy! Year's back he had dreamt of

his wife's assassination and had quickly wanted her not to return to mainstream politics-but who can evade fate. Who can go against the wishes of Allah! He opened his eyes to face Prince and held his hand tightly – Allah take my life not my son's, the Ex-PM muttered- Prince nothing will happen to you. A cluster of by standers came to attention alerted by the sound of the Ex-pm. Dr Zaqi came forward to feel the pulse. The Pm was losing out. Zarine ordered one of the maids to fetch some freshly squeezed juice and fruits in case the PM was able to take some nourishment, and dismissed the rest. The room fell silent again, but after a moment or two, they heard in the distance sound of cheering from the Sultan's clan from the avenue outside the Karachi Guv's house. Word had reached the crowd:

Chapter

The PM had regained consciousness. 'A dream' Asif repeated for the third time. He looked up at the prince, who was still massaging his feet. He reached out and touched his son's hand, as if unsure whether he was real or figment of his night mare. 'prince he said slowly, wondering 'My son-Yes Abba, I am right here! Asif raised his eyes to Dr Zaki .A light of hope shone on his pupils .It was a dream after all! Prince and Zarine were still present in the Governor's house. They have-not joined the rest of the party members in the non – cooperation movement launched by senior members of the party. History was repeating itself yet again and for the worse and that's not a good sign. The General had again deposed Asif, a legitimate liberal democratically elected leader. Unfortunately this time he got elected by popular mandate —and that was his mistake .The General who had lost face with the public, CIA and even the terrorist groups whom he had nurtured tried to assassinate him. So, under duress and trying circumstances the General reluctantly had to give up power —to the elected Asif. After coming to power, Asif faced the worst economic recession that jolted the whole world. No wonder, his state did not have the expenses for even a month. Friends did not help. So, he had to literally beg with IMF to bail the state out. His goodwill also earned the help of the neighboring Gandhiland .The PM of Gandhi land came all-out to help the nation. Economic and trade ties were restored   and train lines resumed .The two nations also committed to no first use of nuclear weapons ,and to sort out all outstanding problems under a new pact .Even the two nations decided to hold a cricket match in the ensuing month. So, generally the two nations were coming close in a big way. A different perception was developing on both sides an atmosphere of Aman or friendship. And suddenly the terrorists attacked Mumbai, all of them belonging to Sultanland and biggest ever such attack on Gandhi land. The Generals had again taken their revenge. Their insecurity had led to this ghastly attack. All the terrorists involved in the ghastly attack had been training for a long time inside Pak territory and Pak army trainers to hit it big .The PM of Gandhiland was supposed to be there in one of the hotels that was attacked. The main reason behind the same attack was to humiliate and draw the peaceful Gandhi land into war –so that the Sultan land army can seize power in the name of war and anarchy .They are not bothered what the cost will be and what impact it will have on their states' s already fragile economy . And they were sure that in the case of a war they will bully the CIA to support them or else they will withdraw their support from WATA. The General /ISI were ready to take the risk even though their ill adventure have resulted in severe loss of face and utter humiliation at the hands of Gandhi land armed forces again and again. The   army /the General and ISI are in state of self-denial and averse to lies .They have fed the majority of Sultan land to believe that the 1965 war when Gandhi land attacked and captured Lahore and the war was actually won by them. And even shamelessly they celebrate it as Defense Day and have declared it as a national Holiday. Such is their state of self-denial. However the terrorist attack did not have the consent of the PM. What can he do? He saw the whole drama unfolding before him. The government became so fractured that what the constitutional head proposes (Such as sending the ISI chief to Gandhi land is summarily disposed by what is technically just government's order, then that government does not deserve to remain in place. After all not only does the civilian Government lack any political control, it lacks any theoretical legitimacy. In 1918 German sociologist Max Weber defined the state as "An entity with the monopoly over the legitimate use of violence" Bhutoland today; there are three types of violence that are beyond the purview of the local police: Violence by terrorists and extremists both within their land and outside it, Violence by CIA armed forces upon their land, Violence by PAK army against the terrorist, tribal Pashtu's and rebel Balochs.   The civilian Government has zero say in any serious decision making therefore it has zero legitimacy. Though Asif's government had been talking peace from the moment he came to power, such an emasculated entity cannot deliver on its transparently genuine intention. So there is no point in pursuing the peace agenda, which he realized sooner than later that he was the de jure ruler, who was made to handle international pressure and domestic problems but his responsibilities came without any rights.   The terrorist attacks impact coupled with the economic quagmire jolted him. Even he had threatening phone calls by the defense minister of Gandhi land threatening war. On the face of it Asif was giving statements blaming the attack and committed that he will bring the culprits under punitive action. He started all this by banning the terror outfits and arresting some of the terrorist leaders involved. The government crackdown was first of its kind in their state. Suddenly ,a part of the army, police and the establishment got cold to such arrests -the radicals came out in large numbers and without half the establishment who had been Talibanised not responding –within a week Sultan land was in chaos and cities were burning with anti-Government protests. History

repeated itself .The army again took
over.

Chapter

The General was in National news-supported though reluctantly by CIA. Did they have a choice? The action was Swift – the PM was detained in the Karachi Governors house. The PM's intelligence informed that he might be assassinated. The PM becomes restive he was surrounded by party seniors in the bungalow with the General's security person's outside .The PM makes an important call in his Secret cell phone. The party council decided that that PM who was sinking had to be airlifted to his farm house residence in the outskirt of London, for two reasons-one to regain his health and most importantly, his own country had become unsafe for him.   Zarine received a call in her international Cell phone and was literally whispering to someone important on the other side of the cell phone. Prince knew he had to act fast and control the restive crowd or else things would be out of control!Meanwhile, Prince darted through the crowds like a swallow through a thicket. The crowds outside the Karachi Governors 's house was dense and growing denser by the second ,but still there was enough space between them to allow a slender youth to slip through if he was quick and agile. All through his movements towards the avenue ,the Captains attention had been diverted by the noisy crowds, that made Prince job to reach the crowds somehow easier .Prince had decided the house arrest was no simple detention- he had received a secret

SMS from an unknown friend. He had already sensed the Generals coup and his sixth sense said something dangerous was in the offing. So, before the general's stooges reach Karachi, he had the responsibility to warn the crowds –to turn to them to his father's support -may be for the last time. He had embarked on this thought out of an impulse- the PM or his aides had no idea of his intention. It was some kind of Adesh from Allah! Now, he ran like his life depended on it .The crowds bustling, excited people were too entranced with discussing the events of that morning to pay him any attention .Those that did glance his way saw merely a handsomely constructed young man in a hurry .He was on foot ,running like a maniac, and carried no weapons or obvious marks of his lineage, just the simple Lee jeans and a black T-shirt with the sign of his foreign university insignia in the back. Nobody recognized him instantly, and those that had a flutter of a doubt were unable to take a second look to check. In moments, he had crossed that swirling river of humanity that the avenue had become .Reaching the end of the concourse; he slowed, seeing the familiar glint of Ak-47s. A road block. Prince spoke to the captain of the unit .What happened here?

Chapter

The Captain spoke without turning back. On your way citizen .This is state business. Prince raised his hands and clasped at the captain's shoulders –Akram is that you? Captain Akram turns back to a call familiar to him. Well he was shocked to see the PM's son in the crowd. The happy contours in his lips –gave way to severe contrition on his face.What the hell are you doing here Baba? Trouble has been brewing since the PM's detention; we are not sure who the PM's supporter is as we can sense hard line supporters of the general are moving around. 'I would request you to immediately turnaround and reach the Governors' house, before you are noticed "

.Akram," I have come out knowing the danger to my life –however it is make or break in this situation .Can you arrange a bit of security around the college podium. So that I can address the crowd". Before, Akram could reply prince was on the St.stephen's college podium-raising his hands to attract attention. Someone from the crowd below shouted –that is prince –the PM's son! All hell broke loose .Some wanted to shake hands, some wanted to touch him .All of a sudden captain Akram sprang into action –he summoned eight of his tallest policemen of Baloch race to surround the prince. Prince was trying to tell something but it was lost in the crowed .Out of nowhere some bearded men materialized near the podium One of them was trying to come up –but was pulled down by part of the crowd .Soon a mini scuffle started- that seemed to be running out of control.

Chapter

Captain Akram realized Prince's life was in danger. Akram eyes met prince's eyes .What's princes got him into now? And how's he going to get out of it? It was not there schools rugby field, that Prince can give the slip .So what? Prince is the real Prince.   Prince started singing the ancient anthem. It took Akram a moment to realize what he was hearing but when Prince began to sing,

Akram understood what he was trying to achieve. Unable to appeal to the two clashing groups with logic and commands, Prince was resorting to patriotic emotion. When he began; the two factions had started shouting war cries and had raised an ominous duet of doom. Above this dark symphony, there now rose the melodious anthem of ancient Aryan clans.   Prince's voice was a clear tenor patriotic emotion. Above this dark symphony, there now rose the melodious anthem of ancient clans Prince's voice was a clear tenor with perfect pitch and just enough bass to lend it depth. As he sang the opening lines, his hand and neck rise as the Captain instantly felt the change in the atmosphere. The ancient anthem had great powers, believed by some to turn desert lands fertile and calm the most ferocious of predators of the wild. Even if those   were exaggerations, the power of the anthem on the mobs ears was undeniable.   Akram could feel the shackles breaking as Prince sang the beautiful, stirring words that praised the mighty subcontinent that housed the ancient noble clans, addressing the land that nourished and provided for them, their mother. The crowd was startled by the ancient chants. It shook their roots as they were not exposed to these ancient Vedic chants it was strange for them , yet it was still there in their consciousness as they were the followers of sanatan dharma for thousands of years , though they had been converted to Islam not long back.

Prince was a devote Muslim. Yet his grandmother though converted, read the Koran along with the Vedas! King Akbar was a devout Muslim but his Hindu wives practiced the tenets of Hinduism. So this tradition of mutual respect and tolerance is quite old in this ancient land. From his early formative years he had grown up with these ancient chants- that praised their land and nature and their forefathers. Obviously the chants though strange were having a tremendous impact on the restless crowd. Slowly some from the crowds started picking up the rhythms and started humming to Prince's song. As they approached the second verse, Akram felt something strange and wonderful happen .it was as if a giant cloud had been pressing down on the whole concourse all this time, making every one uneasy and restless, and some violent and agitated, with the singing of the ancient Vedic song , Akram felt the evil clouds begin to lift. And then he felt an even more wonderful thing. Others were singing too. Stray soldiers in the captains rank voices rising uncertainly   from the bearded mob. And further away, around the corner and up the avenue, past the cordon of police veterans, the citizen were picking up the song too. Like all ancient chants this one had a way of touching your heart no matter who you were, where you were ,or what you were doing at the time.   For those few moments ,everyone in the crowd young or old ,rich or poor ,male or female ,liberal or hard liner , was united in a bond as ancient and undeniable as their mutual dependence on the gift of food and life that the earth mother provided. The ancient song came to an end .There was a brief   moment   of   deafening emptiness .And then, it was all over.

Elsewhere, the general cried out with rage and threw the papers stand at the big 3-D TV on the wall. The action was so swift and sudden that all members of the army council were startled as the glass on the TV broke loose and fell shattering to the floor with a thunderous sound-as if a gunshot had been fired. The happenings at Karachi's St.Stephens College square had shattered his confidence. The general was fuming hot. An unbreakable pain rose in his stomach as he clutched himself he tried to understand what had gone wrong. He had thought it such a clever plan, to use the hardliners who were anti-PM to start the riots which would result in a swift assassination. Things had gone so well.

The two opposing sides had squared off against each other and were on the verge of a blood bath, the police had been informed to stay neutral. The killing of a hard liner by police bullet would have set the stage .A major civilian riot would have broken out. The world media would have believed that civilian riots killed the PM.

'Prince'! Yes prince had come into the picture. And he had spoiled everything. He still did not understand how he had done it. By singing an ancient song? That was ridiculous? How could people be moved by stupid patriotic songs? What was a country anyway? Was it not a land occupied by different people? What was there to get so emotional about? Yet he had done it. Had broken and defied his power. A boy of 19 had spoiled his plans. The general's sixth sense told him this boy will go a long way.

Chapter

Confidential Information

10.30-1st-Two stealth Gandhi land hover crafts -F-36 -30 commandos leave a hidden airfield in Surratt.   12.30-1st-They have landed at an unused airport at Karachi.   1.30-1st-Two stealth Hover crafts reach Governor's house Karachi

2.00-1st-Pm, Chief aids of staff and 20 close aides leave Governor's House for an undisclosed airport.   2.30-1st am- Prince & Zarine leave for airport in the second craft. 2.45-1st-   F-30 flies off with the PM, Prince, Zarine and 8 close aides for an undisclosed location. 2.55-1st- operations   successful. 3.001[st]-   NG-gets the green   signal.   3.00-1st- General   is   alerted   of development.   3.101[st]- Bhutoland F-18 give chase but unsuccessful.   01/01/2009- Bhutto Farmhouse-21 miles from London. Prince& Zarine address world press.   Time 9.Pm

Chapter

Two years later. Prince was in the library of Edinburgh , two monks approached him and handed over a letter to him, it was a confidential letter   from the Head Lama inviting him to Base Zero. He had been waiting for this invitation since the last six   months.

He packed his bags and along with the monk took the cab to the airport ! They have to reach Kathmandu and from there to Kashmir!

Years later, in the ensuing revolt , the General was assassinated . Most of his core staff was killed systematically! The General 's family had escaped to china and had been given refuge in Shanghai as he had personal investments there with money siphoned away from World

Bank Funds , Funds given by US for fighting their proxy wars , from IMF for flood relief - all funds went to Shanghai - investment in China. Shanghai has become the new Swiss Banks to stash illegal money and place for illegal investment. Prince , along with Adwait had assisted Zarine with organizing the revolt. After elections her party was the popular party as they had led the struggle to free the country from the rule of the evil General.

She had been supported by Gandhi land and Americana. In the meanwhile Bhutto land under Zarine had become the leader of the Islamic states.   And she had a big role in bringing about peace in the Middle East and other Islamic states. Israel, under the persuasion of Americana, Bhutto land and Gandhi land had accepted the state of Palestine. Iran on its part had left its hawkish attitude and signed the treaty of no first use of nuclear weapons. The Islamic nations were pulling together as single bloc, enjoying trade ties, exchange of technologies, health sector, education sector, and infrastructure. AS oil resource was on the verge of exhaustion, the gulf nations were looking for alternate ways of income and investment.   Yet the discovery of shale oil in Gandhi land had brought about a paradigm shift in world politics. The Gulf nations had converted their towns into international banking towns for MNC's, while some cities were in the process of building International Trading Houses with state of the art facilities. To accommodate the foreigners the Gulf Nations had adopted laws conforming to international norms and traditions.

And they had set International schools, technical schools with collaboration with technical Institutes of Gandhi land. Students from all over the   world flocked to this new Educational hub, which was based on the ancient Gurukul System.

They had also started many advanced health centres, with the best facilities that one can expect, with professionals running them. So all this was happening under the leadership of Zarine, helped by Adwait the Ruler of Gandhiland. Extremism had been rooted out in all these nations, as   peace and development became the buzzword. Gandhiland had become a huge economic power, and it was following an open economic system and was in a way assisting   its neighbouring nations, economically and was the major consultant in education, technology and health.

So under Zarine Bhutto land had shed its past and was now on the way up politically, socially and economically. And in a way its friendship with

Gandhi land was helping its cause, as it shed its insecurity and   left the negative friendship of nations that exploited it and destroyed it. And the best thing that happened was that Bhutto land and Gandhi land had signed a treaty – at Wagah Boder, Known as the Wagah Boder Treaty, which changed the border posts from posts of war to posts of peace and exchange.   People   could   now crossover to either side without any official   hindrances.   Exchange   of people greatly impacted the growth of both   the   nations   towards   better understanding   and   positive development. Many   students   from Bhutto land flocked to Gandhi land to pursue higher studies. Cultural sites were a big draw in both nations and in a way it united both the Nations. Gandhi land's positive role in its neighborhood had in a way controlled the negativity of nations like China land and North Korea, simmering discontent was spreading in these closed nations, and it was long before a major revolution was   on its way. People are not allowed to travel outside their nations in these nations, as the government fears people going abroad may not come back, and you can't blame them, it has been the standard practice. It's really sad that Nations like these exit where there is no respect for human rights. A nation which does not have faith in its own citizen, what kind of Nation is it? The Chinese have illegally taken over Tibet, and even Tibet is out of bounds for the Chinese as they fear their citizens will know the atrocities they are carrying out there. A holy land and holy rule has been destroyed, definitely there will be day when it will pay   for this misadventure, and it will become another   Bangladesh or even Afghanistan.

As for now as peace and stability have returned to Middle east, Bhutto land and Gandhi land, under the leadership of Adwait and Zarine, the MNCs of Americana and Europia had started operations in these areas. They had impressed international opinion to stop operations in China land. Though a few were still were continuing out of greed to tap the Chinese market. But the world was moving away from China land. Majority of the Nations had ceased relationship with China land, and it had a great impact on it economy, sporadic rebellions were   Common, sending the signals of things to come.

The Tibetans had launched an aggressive attack on all Chinese installations all over the world, bringing an end to all its foreign embassies and trading points. The end of the brutal regime was not far away.

End Of Book Two

www.ingramcontent.com/pod-product-compliance
Lightning Source LLC
Chambersburg PA
CBHW021015160726
47994CB00006B/2525